written by:
TRILLIA NEWBELL

illustrated by:
CATALINA ECHEVERRI

the BIG wide WELCOME

Art and Activity Book

PACKED WITH PUZZLES AND ACTIVITIES!

The Big Wide Welcome Art and Activity Book
© The Good Book Company 2022

"The Good Book For Children" is an imprint of The Good Book Company Ltd
North America: www.thegoodbook.com UK: www.thegoodbook.co.uk
Australia: www.thegoodbook.com.au New Zealand: www.thegoodbook.co.nz
India: www.thegoodbook.co.in

Created and illustrated by Jorie Lee Design, based on the original story by
Trillia Newbell and original illustrations by Catalina Echeverri.
Cover design and art direction by André Parker

ISBN US: 9781784987886 UK: 9781802540444 | Printed in India

Let's play favorites!
Do you have a
favorite food?

Draw your favorite
food here.

Do you have a favorite toy?
A favorite superhero?
A favorite teddy?

We all have favorite things. It's fine
to play favorites like this...

... unless we play favorites with people. That is a big problem.

It isn't a new problem. It's a very old problem. A long time ago, in the Bible, a church leader called James wanted some Christians to think hard about it.

Spot the difference

So he told them a story...

Can you spot the 6 differences in these pictures of James writing to some Christians?

Imagine (wrote James) that it's a
Sunday and you're all in church.
And then in walks a really rich man.

Here's what they did.

Then imagine (wrote James) that
a poor man walks in.

Here's what they did.

This church was playing favorites based on how much money people had. They gave a big welcome to people who had lots, but they had no welcome for people who had little.

Draw a picture of the rich man lying in a pile of gold.

But (wrote James) rich people weren't better than poorer people. Some of those rich people were being mean to Christians. Some of them did not love Jesus.

And although poor people did not have much money, many of them did love Jesus. They had treasures upon treasures and a big wide welcome waiting for them in heaven.

Draw a picture of the poor man lying in a field of grass.

So (James wrote), don't play favorites. Instead, choose to love.

Like those churches, we might treat people better because they have more money. And we can play favorites with people in other ways, too.

But in the Bible James said, *Don't play favorites; choose to love.*

Maze

Help the kids choose the path that can lead to showing love instead of playing favorites.

Wordsearch

h	K	K	r	e	x	s	s	j	i	s	t	u	p	u
g	h	a	t	z	i	f	s	u	e	p	o	o	r	y
e	f	r	i	e	n	d	t	h	t	s	t	g	a	d
l	w	l	j	a	s	w	e	n	l	l	r	e	f	v
j	a	m	e	s	f	y	e	r	g	e	e	s	a	t
s	e	o	s	e	h	r	e	s	t	t	a	d	v	b
r	d	w	s	e	e	f	e	m	o	t	s	u	o	k
m	o	b	e	f	a	n	o	r	l	e	u	d	r	a
e	K	h	f	i	r	o	w	i	e	r	r	e	i	w
s	l	i	d	f	t	c	K	c	t	n	e	c	t	n
s	d	m	g	e	s	y	j	h	s	u	t	m	e	d
a	i	i	s	t	o	r	y	o	d	y	c	s	k	n
g	b	f	i	v	e	s	a	g	f	s	K	o	w	n
e	o	n	e	t	t	e	l	o	y	l	o	v	e	l
s	c	h	u	r	c	h	x	g	r	i	t	r	f	a

☐ James   ☐ church   ☐ different

☐ story   ☐ friend   ☐ heart

☐ rich   ☐ wrote   ☐ love

☐ poor   ☐ favorite   ☐ treasure

When Jesus, the Son of God, walked on the earth as a man, he talked to all sorts of people.

He talked to rich people and to poor people.

Jesus talked to people who had darker skin and to people who had lighter skin.

Color these people all differently.

He talked to sick people.

Join the dots

Join the dots to see where this man is.

Start at 1 and
join the dots.

Jesus talked to people who everyone else
chose not to talk to.

Why?

Because Jesus loves all people.

Jesus knew that everyone was in trouble because they had decided not to live with God as their Savior and Friend. Jesus knew that everyone needed him to rescue them.

Jesus didn't play favorites...

... Jesus chose to LOVE!

In fact, Jesus loves people so much that he chose to die on the cross so that all people could be friends with him. Jesus welcomes as his friend anyone who asks to be his friend!

Maze

Solve the maze to lead people
to the cross.

And that means...

You can be friends with Jesus, too!

... you are good at sports
... you look great or wear cool stuff
... you are smart
... you behave well

Jesus chooses to love

you!

James says, *If you're friends with Jesus, be like Jesus.* Jesus doesn't want you to play favorites with people. He wants you to love people like he loves people.

Our churches should be big-wide-welcome places — places where there are no favorites, and everyone is loved.

Draw or write about a way you can make others feel welcome.

Wordsearch

r	K	i	g	b	h	s	a	g	e	s	c	u	e	u
e	w	e	l	c	o	m	e	p	l	c	e	p	c	y
s	i	i	r	e	t	n	u	h	l	r	r	o	h	d
c	s	r	d	p	a	r	K	r	o	a	y	o	o	v
h	c	d	y	e	r	e	s	j	h	a	n	d	s	t
o	i	o	e	i	a	r	t	a	e	u	l	i	e	s
o	p	l	t	c	m	b	p	h	o	s	d	y	v	K
l	l	i	r	i	i	h	e	y	e	y	u	r	e	r
l	e	l	u	e	s	d	t	l	i	r	i	s	e	t
a	s	w	r	e	c	K	e	r	o	r	s	v	b	h
z	j	h	j	w	r	l	i	r	e	e	e	m	c	h
c	h	o	o	s	e	a	l	i	v	o	a	e	r	o
e	j	w	u	w	n	e	y	g	h	t	t	c	i	m
g	g	t	e	t	h	a	l	w	a	y	s	g	i	e
s	f	o	y	r	i	a	h	s	s	o	r	c	f	b

☐ Jesus   ☐ wow   ☐ you

☐ choose   ☐ decide   ☐ school

☐ cross   ☐ always   ☐ park

☐ welcome   ☐ whoever   ☐ home

Match the shadows

Can you match these people to their shadows?

You can be like Jesus
wherever you are...

At school.
Playing sports.
At home.
In the park.

You can decide,
"I won't play favorites –
I will choose to love."

Draw a
picture of
yourself.

And most of all, you can remember that
Jesus doesn't play favorites. And that means
that, wherever you are and whoever you are,
Jesus loves YOU!

Answers

Spot the difference

Maze 1

a

b

c

Wordsearch 1

h	k	k	r	e	x	s	s	j	i	s	t	u	p	u
g	h	a	t	z	i	f	s	u	e	p	o	o	r	y
e	f	r	i	e	n	d	t	h	t	s	t	g	a	d
l	w	l	j	a	s	w	e	n	l	l	r	e	f	v
j	a	m	e	s	f	y	e	r	g	e	e	s	a	t
s	e	o	s	e	h	r	e	s	t	t	a	d	v	b
r	d	w	s	e	e	f	e	m	o	t	s	u	o	k
m	o	b	e	f	a	n	o	r	l	e	u	d	r	a
e	k	h	f	i	r	o	w	i	e	r	r	e	i	w
s	l	i	d	f	t	c	k	c	t	n	e	c	t	n
s	d	m	g	e	s	y	j	h	s	u	t	m	e	d
a	i	i	s	t	o	r	y	o	d	y	c	s	k	n
g	b	f	i	v	e	s	a	g	f	s	k	o	w	n
e	o	n	e	t	t	e	l	o	y	l	o	v	e	l
s	c	h	u	r	c	h	x	g	r	i	t	r	f	a

Join the dots

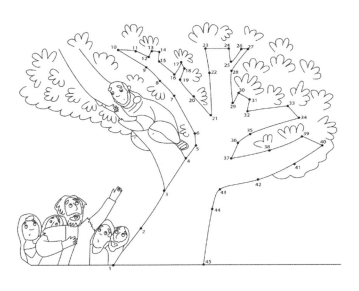

Maze 2

Wordsearch 2

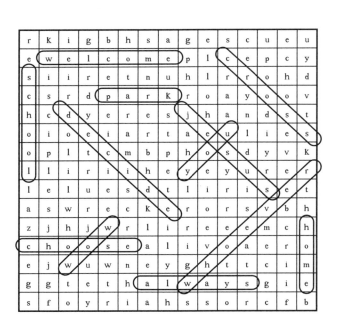

Match the shadows

Now read the book!

If you enjoyed this activity book, read the full story in "The Big Wide Welcome."

Other books available in the
award-winning "Tales That
Tell The Truth" series:

thegoodbook.com   thegoodbook.co.uk